READING POWER

> Sports History <

The Story of Football

Anastasia Suen

Published in 2002 by The Rosen Publishing Group, Inc.
29 East 21st Street, New York, NY 10010

First Edition

Book Design: Christopher Logan

Photo Credits: Cover, pp. 12–17, 20–21 © Bettmann/Corbis; pp. 4–5 © Hulton-Deutsch Collection/Corbis; pp. 6–7 © Oscar White/Corbis; pp. 8–11, 18 © Underwood & Underwood/Corbis; p. 11 (inset) © Corbis; p. 19 © EISA/AllSport; p. 21 (top inset) © Reuters NewMedia Inc./Corbis; p. 21 (bottom inset) © Jamie Squire/AllSport

Suen, Anastasia.
The story of football / by Anastasia Suen.
    p. cm. — (Sports history)
Includes bibliographical references (p.   ) and index.
ISBN 0-8239-5996-1 (lib. bdg.)
1. Football—History—Juvenile literature. [1. Football—History.] I. Title.
GV950.7 .S84 2001
796.332'0973—dc21
                                        2001000592

Manufactured in the United States of America

Contents

The Early Years

American football comes from the game of rugby. Rugby started in England in the 1820s.

Rugby players huddle as a group to push the ball toward the goal.

In 1874, a college rugby team from Canada taught U.S. students at Harvard University how to play the game.

The Harvard students liked rugby, but they wanted to change some of the rules. In 1875, Harvard played Yale University in a game using the new rules. It was the first football game ever played. Soon, other colleges also wanted to play.

Harvard plays Yale in the first football game.

College football games became very popular. Fans liked to go to games because the players lived in their towns. Big crowds made football the most popular college sport.

Big crowds enjoyed watching football games.

IT'S A FACT!

College games were once 70 minutes long. In 1906, the games were changed to 60 minutes.

In the early years, football was a very rough game. Many players got hurt. Players could even punch each other.

Players did not wear much padding in the early years. One player in this picture is not even wearing a helmet.

President Theodore Roosevelt almost made playing football against the law because so many people were getting hurt.

IT'S A FACT!

In 1905, 18 students were killed and more than 150 students were injured playing college football.

Professional Leagues

In 1920, the first professional football league was formed. It was called the American Professional Football Association. In 1922, the name was changed to the National Football League (NFL).

Number of Professional Football Teams

1920:   11 teams

2001:   32 teams

Red Grange was one of the first stars of the NFL.

The 1958 NFL championship game helped make football more popular than ever before. For the first time, football became an important sport on television. People wanted to see even more teams play football. In 1960, the American Football League (AFL) was formed.

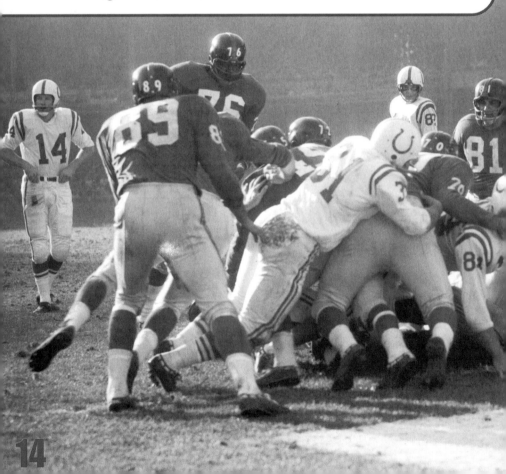

The Baltimore Colts beat the New York Giants in the 1958 NFL championship game. The fans called this "the greatest game ever."

The Super Bowl

In 1967, the first Super Bowl was played between the two best teams from the NFL and the AFL. The Green Bay Packers of the NFL beat the Kansas City Chiefs of the AFL. In 1970, the AFL joined the NFL to make one league.

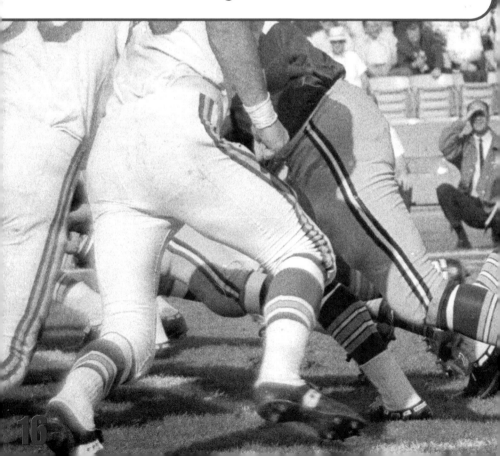

Changes in Equipment

Over the years, there have been many changes in the equipment used by football players. Today's players wear more padding than the players of the past.

Uniform from 1920

Today's players must wear helmets, too. The changes in equipment have been made to protect the players and to make the games more exciting.

Modern uniform

The Game Today

Football is one of the most popular sports in the world. Millions of people love this American game of action.

Glossary

championship (**cham**-pea-uhn-shihp) a contest to determine a winner

equipment (ih-**kwihp**-muhnt) the outfits and supplies that are used for a game

league (**leeg**) a group of sports clubs or teams

padding (**pad**-ihng) soft material worn for protection

professional (pruh-**fehsh**-uh-nuhl) making a business out of what others do for fun

rugby (**ruhg**-bee) a game similar to football

Super Bowl (**soo**-puhr **bohl**) the championship game of the National Football League

Resources

Books

Eyewitness: Football
by James Buckley, Jr.
Dorling Kindersley Publishing (1999)

Gladiators: 40 Years of Football
by Walter Iooss, photographer
Total/Sports Illustrated (2000)

Web Site
National Football League
http://www.nfl.com

Index

Word Count: 342

Note to Librarians, Teachers, and Parents

If reading is a challenge, Reading Power is a solution! Reading Power is perfect for readers who want high-interest subject matter at an accessible reading level. These fact-filled, photo-illustrated books are designed for readers who want straightforward vocabulary, engaging topics, and a manageable reading experience. With clear picture/text correspondence, leveled Reading Power books put the reader in charge. Now readers have the power to get the information they want and the skills they need in a user-friendly format.